PLACES AND PEOPLE

Southeast Asia

Anita Ganeri

Franklin Watts
New York • Chicago • London • Toronto • Sydney

© 1995 Watts Books

Franklin Watts
95 Madison Avenue
New York
NY 10016

10 9 8 7 6 5 4 3 2 1

Library of Congress Cataloging-in-Publication Data
Ganeri, Anita, 1961-
      Southeast Asia / Anita Ganeri
          p. cm. — (Places and people)
      Includes index.
      ISBN 0-531-14367-8
      1. Asia, Southeastern—Juvenile literature. I. Title.
      II. Series.
      DS521.C36   1995   95-11407
      915.9—dc20   CIP AC

Series consultant: Keith Lye
Editor: Jane Walker
Design: Ron Kamen, Green Door Design Ltd.
Cover design: Mike Davis
Maps: Mainline Design
          Visual Image
Additional artwork: Mainline Design
                          Visual Image
Cover artwork: Raymond Turvey
Fact checking: Christine Stockwell
Research: Jonardon Ganeri
Picture research: Alison Renwick, Steve Rowling

Photographic credits (t = top, m = middle, b = bottom): J. Allan Cash: 7, 9, 17(b). Andes
Press Agency: 13(b), 23 Ceri and Dave Hill. Chris Fairclough Colour Library: 21, 26.
Robert Harding Picture Library: 10, 29; 22, 25 Nigel Blythe; 19 Paolo Koch; 18 Julia
Thorne; 28 Paul Van Riel. Hutchison Library: 17(t); 5(b) Guidicelli. ZEFA: 5(t), 13 (t);
15 Hugh Ballantyne; 6 F. Lanting; 14 K. H. Oster; 11 SUNAK.

Printed in Belgium

Contents

Ten nations — Southeast Asia

The region known as Southeast Asia consists of a main peninsula and thousands of islands to the east and south of the peninsula. Southeast Asia occupies about one tenth of the giant continent of Asia.

The region known as Southeast Asia lies to the east of Bangladesh and India and to the south of China. It consists of two peninsulas and thousands of islands. Southeast Asia is made up of ten countries: Brunei, Cambodia, Malaysia, Singapore, Vietnam, Burma (officially called Myanmar), Laos, the Philippines, Thailand, and Indonesia.

The region covers an area of some 1.7 million square miles (4.5 million sq km), surrounded by 4.6 million square miles (12 million sq km) of sea. It is home to around 460 million people, who make up nearly one tenth of the world's population.

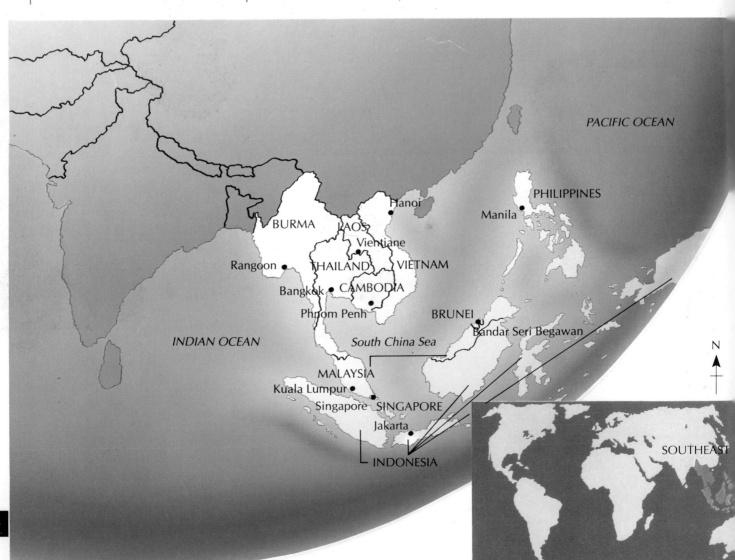

PACIFIC OCEAN

PHILIPPINES

Manila

Hanoi

BURMA

LAOS

Vientiane

Rangoon

THAILAND

VIETNAM

Bangkok

CAMBODIA

Phnom Penh

BRUNEI

Bandar Seri Begawan

INDIAN OCEAN

South China Sea

MALAYSIA

Kuala Lumpur

Singapore   SINGAPORE

Jakarta

INDONESIA

SOUTHEAST

N

Cultural contrasts

Southeast Asia is one of the most complex and diverse places on earth. Its people belong to many different ethnic groups with their own cultures, languages, and religions. The people of this region are descended from the traders, invaders, and settlers who were drawn to Southeast Asia over thousands of years.

The region is full of economic contrasts, too. On the one hand is the tiny but very prosperous island of Singapore; on the other are Laos and Vietnam, which are two of the world's poorest countries. Yet various similarities bind the region together. The countries share a tropical monsoon climate, for example. The economies of Southeast Asia are largely agricultural, and each country depends on rice as its staple food crop. More than half of the people are Buddhists, and most are generally fairly poor.

A history of war

For centuries, Southeast Asia has been a center of war and upheaval as foreign powers have attempted to gain control of the region and of its natural resources. There have also been conflicts between various ethnic groups within and between individual countries. Since the end of World War II in 1945, both Vietnam and Cambodia have suffered terribly. Between 1965 and 1975, the United States fought the Vietnam War to prevent the spread of Communism in Southeast Asia. In the late 1970s, two million Cambodians are believed to have been killed under the brutal Communist government led by the Khmer Rouge organization. In both these conflicts, millions of people were killed, injured, made homeless, or forced to flee their country.

The modern skyline of Singapore (top) and a village street in rural Laos (bottom) are two contrasting images of Southeast Asia.

Islands and highlands

Southeast Asia is made up of two peninsulas and thousands of islands. Burma, Laos, Vietnam, Cambodia, Thailand, and the western part of Malaysia form the mainland of Southeast Asia. Eastern Malaysia consists of two states, Sabah and Sarawak, on the island of Borneo. Another part of Borneo forms the tiny country of Brunei. The remainder of the island, and over 13,600 other islands, make up Indonesia, which is the largest archipelago in the world. The Philippines is another nation of islands, with over 7,000 in total.

The map (right) shows the principal physical features of Southeast Asia, including its major rivers, numerous islands, and highest mountains.

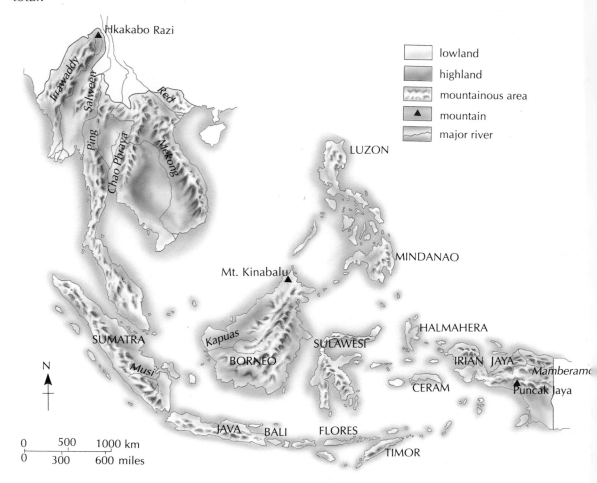

lowland
highland
mountainous area
▲ mountain
major river

A lowland rain forest on the island of Borneo. Forests cover much of the land of Southeast Asia.

Forests, mountains, and volcanoes

Much of Southeast Asia is covered in dense, tropical rain forest and high mountains. The highest point in the region is Hkakabo-razi in Burma 19,295 feet (5,881 m). Other high peaks include Puncak Jaya Indonesia 16,503 feet (5,030 m) and Mount Kinabalu in the Malaysia part of Borneo 13,432 feet (4,094 m). The rain forests once covered a much more extensive area than they do today. Because of excessive logging activities, they are now disappearing rapidly (see page 26).

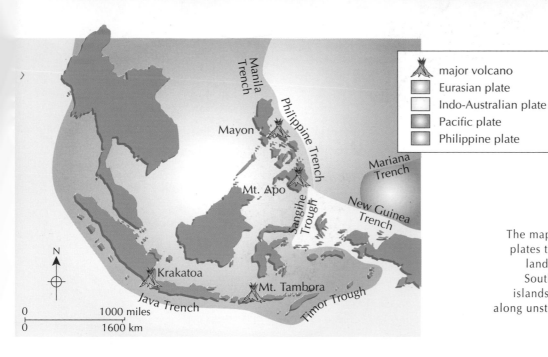

Manila Trench

Mayon

Philippine Trench

Mt. Apo

Mariana Trench

Sangihe Trough

New Guinea Trench

Krakatoa

Java Trench

Mt. Tambora

Timor Trough

N

0   1000 miles
0   1600 km

The map shows the main plates that lie below the land and sea areas of Southeast Asia. Many islands in the region lie along unstable plate edges.

The outer layers of the earth consist of about fifteen large sections, called plates, and several smaller ones. The land forming Southeast Asia lies around the edges of three of these plates. Plates are more unstable around their edges, and, as a result, parts of the region experience frequent earthquakes and a lot of volcanic activity. During the nineteenth and twentieth centuries, some of the world's major earthquakes occurred in this area.

Many of Southeast Asia's mountains and islands were formed by volcanoes. Indonesia alone has over one hundred volcanoes, which is more than any other country in the world. About seventy of its volcanoes are still active. Many of the islands of the Philippines also have active volcanoes.

Rivers and seas

The majority of people in Southeast Asia live along the banks and delta areas of large rivers. The land beside these rivers is fertile and so it is suitable for farming. The region's longest river is the mighty Mekong. It flows more than 2,484 miles (4,000 km) from its source in the mountains of Tibet, China, to its densely populated delta in southern Vietnam.

The sea has helped to shape both the region's geography and its culture. Southeast Asia has a longer coastline that any other region of a similar size. This means that outsiders have been able to travel across the sea and reach easily the countries of Southeast Asia. Laos is the only landlocked country in the region.

The Mekong River (below) forms much of the border between Laos and Thailand.

Monsoons and typhoons

Southeast Asia lies on either side of the equator. Most of the region shares a tropical climate, which means that the weather is hot and humid all year around. The region's climate is dominated by the arrival of the monsoon winds, which bring heavy rains. These rains are essential for the farmers and their crops. In particular, the rains are needed for the all-important rice crop, which thrives in wet, warm conditions. Average temperatures across the region, and throughout the year, are around 79°F (26°C). Temperatures are lower in the mountainous areas, becoming cooler the higher up the mountains you travel.

Winds and rains

Monsoons are winds that change direction according to the time of year. In both Burma and Thailand, the violent thunderstorms that mark the start of the monsoon season are known as "mango rains." From May to October, the southwest monsoon brings torrential rain to Burma, Thailand, Malaysia, the Philippines, Vietnam, Cambodia and Laos. In parts of Indonesia, the rainy season lasts from December to March with the arrival of the northeast monsoon.

Throughout much of Southeast Asia, the average amount of rainfall in a year is about 99 inches (250 cm). Failure of the monsoon means drought and disaster for farmers. Yet, at the other extreme, very heavy rains can cause severe flooding that is equally destructive.

The average January and July temperatures and the average annual rainfall for the region's ten capital cities are given below.

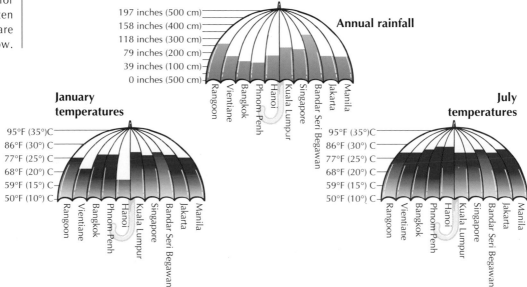

8

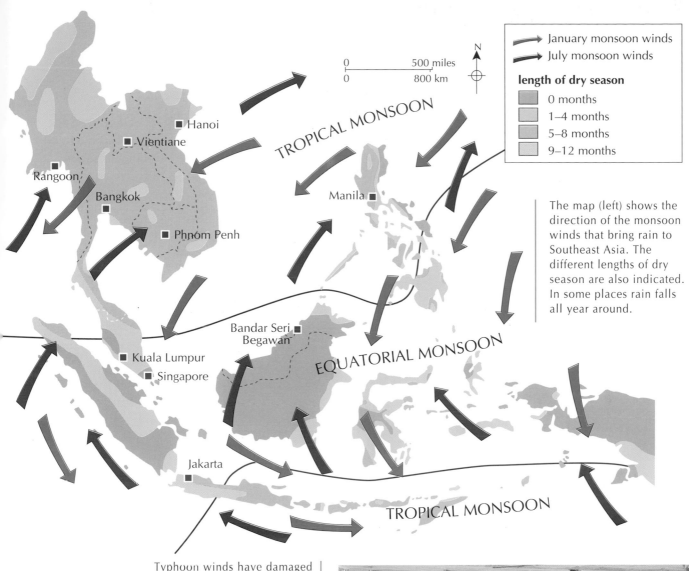

January monsoon winds
July monsoon winds

length of dry season
- 0 months
- 1–4 months
- 5–8 months
- 9–12 months

0   500 miles
0   800 km

N

TROPICAL MONSOON

Hanoi
Vientiane
Rangoon
Bangkok
Phnom Penh
Manila

The map (left) shows the direction of the monsoon winds that bring rain to Southeast Asia. The different lengths of dry season are also indicated. In some places rain falls all year around.

Bandar Seri Begawan
Kuala Lumpur
Singapore

EQUATORIAL MONSOON

Jakarta

TROPICAL MONSOON

Typhoon winds have damaged these banana trees on the island of Luzon in the Philippines.

Typhoon terror

The Philippines lie in the path of violent storms called typhoons. They normally occur between July and October. Typhoons are huge, swirling masses of very strong winds, torrential rains and thick clouds. They occur when heat rises off the warm tropical seas. (In other parts of the world, typhoons are called tropical cyclones or hurricanes.)

Typhoons die down once they reach land but not before they have caused enormous damage to buildings, fields of crops, people, and their homes. In 1984, about 16,000 people died when two typhoons hit the islands of the Philippines.

Many different peoples

The origins of the people who came to settle in Southeast Asia are shown below. Europeans only started to arrive in the region during the 1500s.

Around 460 million people live in Southeast Asia, making the region a very densely populated area. The number of people per square mile (per sq km) is at least ten times higher than the world average. Indonesia, which has a population of over 184 million, is the fifth most populous country in the world (after China, India, the former Soviet Union, and the United States). However, the population is not evenly distributed across the region (see page 12).

New arrivals

The people of Southeast Asia belong to a large number of different ethnic groups. This wide variety stems from the centuries-old influx of traders, workers, and invaders from other parts of the world. The region's long coastline, in particular, has made it highly accessible by sea.

People began to arrive in Southeast Asia from China as early as 3000 B.C. although there were people already living there. Chinese people continue to settle in the region today, and Malaysia and Singapore, for example, have large Chinese populations. From the first century A.D., Indian and Arab traders from India brought their culture and religions to the region. From the sixteenth century onward, most of Southeast Asia was ruled by colonial powers. The Portuguese, the Spanish, the British, the French, and the Dutch added their cultures.

CHINA

INDIA

Arabian Peninsula

BURMA VIETNAM
THAILAND LAOS
CAMBODIA
PHILIPPINES

BRUNEI
MALAYSIA
SINGAPORE

INDONESIA

UK
NETHERLANDS
FRANCE
SPAIN
PORTUGAL

N

0   1000 km
0   600   miles

The ruined temple of Angkor Wat in northwest Cambodia. It was built in the twelfth century near Angkor Thom, capital city of the Angkor civilization.

10

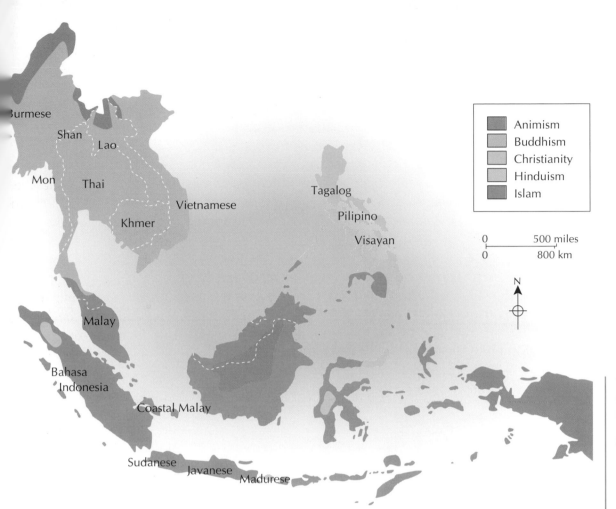

Animism
Buddhism
Christianity
Hinduism
Islam

Burmese
Shan
Lao
Mon
Thai
Khmer
Vietnamese
Tagalog
Pilipino
Visayan
Malay
Bahasa Indonesia
Coastal Malay
Sudanese
Javanese
Madurese

0   500 miles
0   800 km

N

The major religions and principal languages of Southeast Asia.

Language and religion

The languages and religions of Southeast Asia reflect the region's long history of foreign influence. Hundreds of different languages and dialects are spoken, including Chinese, English, and French, which are important second languages.

Four of the world's major religions are practiced in Southeast Asia—Hinduism, Buddhism, Islam, and Christianity. Each was introduced to the region by outsiders. Hinduism arrived in the first century A.D. with merchants and priests from India. Buddhism, the major religion of Burma, Thailand, Laos, Cambodia, and Vietnam, also came from India. Islam was introduced by Arab traders in the thirteenth century. Islam is the major religion of Indonesia, Malaysia, and Brunei, and more than half of the population of these countries are Muslims. Christianity, particularly Roman Catholicism, was brought to the region by the Spanish, the Portuguese, and the French. It is the main religion of the Philippines.

The Shwe Dagon pagoda (below) in the Burmese capital, Rangoon (officially called Yangon). It is one of Burma's best-known Buddhist temples.

Life along the rivers

ivers are the lifeblood of Southeast Asia. They provide lines of communication and a means of transportation. In addition, they are rich sources of fish for local food and export and provide a ready supply of water for the irrigation of the all-important rice crop. Not surprisingly, the region's population is densest along the riverbanks and around the river deltas. Here, regular flooding of the rivers leaves deposits of fertile soil, which is suitable for farming.

Major rivers

Five major rivers run from north to south through the mainland of Southeast Asia. They are the Mekong (in Laos, Cambodia, and southern Vietnam), the Irrawaddy and the Salween (in Burma), the Chao Phraya (in Thailand), and the Red River (in northern Vietnam). The Chao Phraya forms where four separate rivers join together in Thailand's central plain. Burma's Irrawaddy River flows for over 1,300 miles (2,000 km) through the center of the country and out into the Bay of Bengal. Both are major transportation routes.

The population density of Southeast Asia is shown below. Most of the main population centers are found alongside, or close to, one of the region's major rivers.

persons per sq mile (sq km)

- > 3,368 (>1,300)
- 684–3,369 (650–1,30
- 1,010–1,684 (390–65
- 337–1,010 (130–390
- < 337 (<130)

Delta riches

Until the disruption caused by the Vietnam War, the Mekong Delta was one of the greatest rice-producing areas in Southeast Asia. Each year, huge amounts of sediment are deposited by the Mekong along its banks and around the delta. These deposits of mud and sand help to renew the fertility of the soils.

In northern Vietnam, the Red River floods the densely populated delta area each year. The land in the deltas of both these rivers is about 10 feet (3 m) below sea level in places.

Island rivers

On the islands of Southeast Asia and on mainland Malaysia, rivers are much shorter, but they are equally important. Many of the rivers are fastflowing, and so they could provide plentiful hydroelectric power. Their potential has only been partly exploited so far. The rivers are also important transportation routes. In Indonesia, however, they are less important for farming. Here, crops are largely grown in the rich soils that are found around volcanoes.

The Mekong River flows into the sea near Ho Chi Minh City (above), Vietnam's largest city.

Logs are floated down the Mahakan River in eastern Borneo. Rivers provide the island's main transportation routes.

The land of two rice baskets

Vietnam is sometimes called the "land of two rice baskets" because of its shape. The deltas in the north and south of the country resemble two rice baskets on either end of a farmer's carrying pole. (The pole is represented by the long, narrow strip of land between them.) Rice is the most important crop throughout Southeast Asia. It is the staple food crop and also a major export, or cash, crop. The region is one of the largest producers of rice in the world.

The main food crops grown in Southeast Asia. The percentage figure is the amount of land that is used for growing crops in each country.

BURMA
cropland 12%
- rice
- cereals
- peanuts

LAOS
cropland 4%
- rice
- maize
- cassava

VIETNAM
cropland 20%
- rice
- yams
- cassava

THAILAND
cropland 39%
- rice
- maize
- cassava

CAMBODIA
cropland 17%
- rice
- fruits
- maize

INDONESIA
cropland 12%
- rice
- maize
- coconuts

SINGAPORE
cropland 7%
- fruits and vegetables

MALAYSIA
cropland 15%
- rice
- coconuts
- sweet potatoes

BRUNEI
cropland 1.5%
- rice
- cassava
- fruits and vegetables

PHILIPPINES
cropland 27%
- rice
- fruits
- maize

N
0   500 miles
0   800 km

Wet-rice cultivation

The warm, wet climate of Southeast Asia provides ideal growing conditions for rice. Farmers can grow up to three crops of rice each year. Throughout the region, rice is grown in paddy fields where the seedlings are kept standing in water. It takes three to four months for the rice to be ready for harvesting. While the rice plants are growing, the local people perform special rituals and ceremonies to keep the rice goddess happy.

The greatest rice-growing areas are found on the river plains and around the deltas and on the rich volcanic soil of islands such as Java. In mountainous areas, huge, steplike fields, called terraces, are cut into the hillsides. About half of all the cultivated land in Southeast Asia is given over to rice. Other important food crops include cassava, maize, fruits and vegetables.

Most of the region's farmers use traditional farming methods. Rice, for example, is planted and harvested by hand. Instead of using tractors, farmers plow their fields with simple plows pulled by water buffalo.

On the island of Luzon (below), in the Philippines, farmers grow their ce crop on terraces that have been cut into the hillsides.

Southeast Asia 21.5%

rest of world 78.5%

The diagram provides a breakdown of rice production in the world. Southeast Asia produces just over one-fifth of the world's rice supply.

Indonesia	8%
Thailand	4%
Vietnam	3.5%
Burma	3%
Philippines	2%
other Southeast Asian countries	1%

Southeast Asian food

Almost everyone in Southeast Asia eats rice every day, at least once a day. It is the staple food of the region. Fish, both sea and freshwater varieties, is also widely eaten. Many different types of food are eaten in South-East Asia, reflecting the mixture of people that live there. In general, the food is hot and spicy and is often flavored with coconut milk or peanut sauce. Exotic fruits, such as mangoes, pineapples, papayas, and mangosteens, grow well in the tropical climate.

An Indonesian farmer plows his paddy field with the help of a pair of water buffalo.

15

Crops for cash

Many of the crops grown in Southeast Asia are cash crops. These are crops that are grown for export in order to earn valuable foreign currency for the region. The most important cash crops are rubber, palm oil, sugarcane, coconuts and timber, and other products from the tropical rain forests. Indonesia, Malaysia, and Thailand are the world's leading suppliers of rubber. Malaysia is the largest producer of palm oil in the world, followed by Indonesia.

Southeast Asia is a major exporter of tropical fruits, including pineapples, bananas, mangoes, papayas, star fruit, and rambutans. Opium, which is produced from opium poppies, is another important but illegal cash crop. Opium poppies are grown in areas of Burma, Laos, and Thailand.

Spices and plantations

For centuries, precious spices from Southeast Asia were sold by Arab traders to merchants in Europe. The spices included nutmeg, cloves, pepper, and ginger. In the sixteenth century, traders from Europe began to arrive in Southeast Asia to trade directly in spices.

The principal cash (export) crops that are grown in Southeast Asia are shown below.

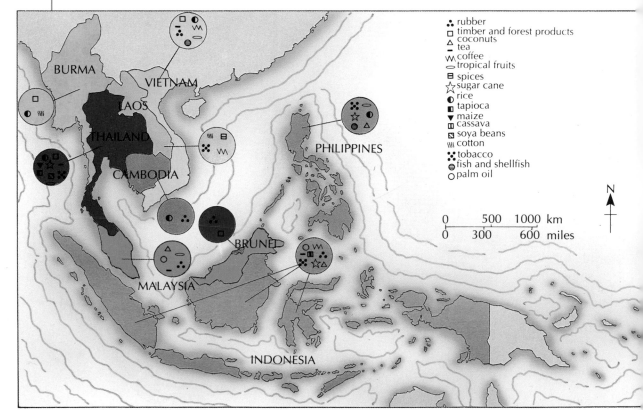

Elephants are used to haul timber in Thailand. Teak is the most important product from Thailand's extensive forests.

By the nineteenth century, colonial rule was firmly established in Southeast Asia. The European settlers brought with them new crops and different farming methods. They set up huge plantations for growing rubber, coffee, palm oil, tobacco, and sugarcane. All these crops had been introduced into Southeast Asia from outside the region.

Timber

About three-quarters of the world's most valuable tropical hardwoods, such as teak, ebony, and mahogany, come from Southeast Asia. These hardwoods grow in the rain forests that cover much of the region. Other important forest products include bamboo and rattan.

However, so many trees have now been cut down that the forests themselves are disappearing at an alarming rate. In an effort to save the rain forests, several countries in the region have banned timber exports. Unfortunately, trees are still being felled illegally, and the timber is then smuggled abroad (see page 26).

Natural rubber is made from a white liquid called latex. The latex is collected from rubber trees by cutting diagonal grooves in the bark (right). It oozes out from the grooves and runs down into a cup below. This method of collecting latex is called "tapping."

Natural resources and industry

S ince regaining independence from the colonial rule of European powers, the industries and economies of many Southeast Asian countries have grown very quickly. Brunei and Singapore are among the world's most prosperous nations. Malaysia, Indonesia, and Thailand are on the United Nations' list of "rapidly industrializing countries." By contrast, Vietnam, Laos, Cambodia, and Burma are some of the world's poorest and least developed countries.

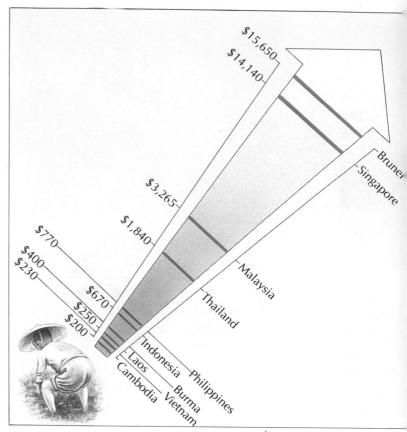

$15,650
$14,140
$3,265
$1,840
$770
$400
$230
$670
$250
$200

Brunei
Singapore
Malaysia
Thailand
Indonesia
Philippines
Laos
Burma
Cambodia
Vietnam

The Gross National Product (GNP) per person for the ten countries of Southeast Asia in the early 1990s. The GNP figures for Brunei and Singapore contrast sharply with those of poor countries like Vietnam and Cambodia.

A wealth of resources?

This rapid economic progress in parts of the region has been made possible by a cheap and plentiful workforce and some sophisticated technology. In addition, most of the region's prosperous countries have a wealth of natural resources. However, strong industrial growth does not necessarily depend on a wealth of natural resources. Singapore, for example, is a leading economic power, yet it has no natural resources. It has to import all the raw materials needed for its "high-tech" industries.

A tribeswoman from northern Thailand producing needlework. Handicrafts such as this are sold to tourists as well as being exported overseas.

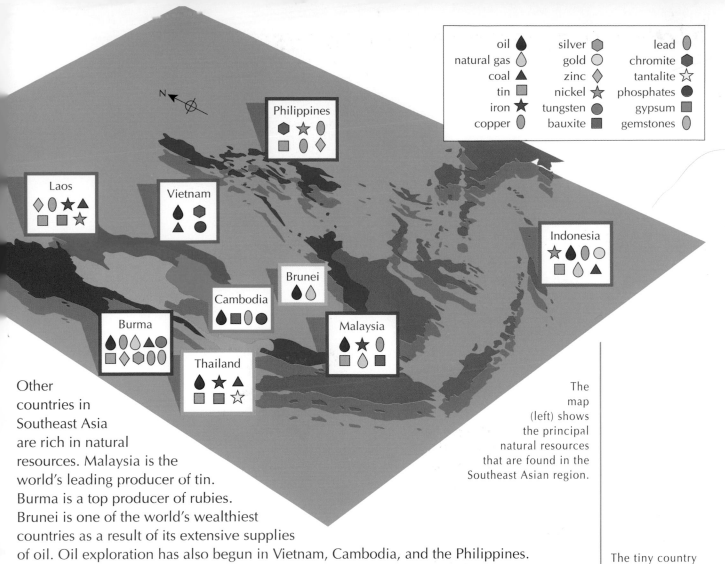

Legend:
- oil ▼
- natural gas ◇
- coal ▲
- tin ■
- iron ★
- copper ○
- silver ⬡
- gold ○
- zinc ◇
- nickel ★
- tungsten ●
- bauxite ■
- lead ○
- chromite ⬣
- tantalite ☆
- phosphates ●
- gypsum ■
- gemstones ○

Philippines ⬣ ★ ○ ■ ○ ◇

Laos ◇ ○ ★ ▲ ■ ■ ☆

Vietnam ▼ ● ▲ ⬣

Brunei ▼ ◇

Cambodia ▼ ■ ○ ● ○

Indonesia ★ ▼ ◇ ○ ■ ◇ ▲

Burma ▼ ○ ◇ ▲ ● ■ ◇ ○ ○

Thailand ▼ ★ ▲ ■ ■ ☆

Malaysia ▼ ★ ○ ■ ◇ ■

The map (left) shows the principal natural resources that are found in the Southeast Asian region.

Other countries in Southeast Asia are rich in natural resources. Malaysia is the world's leading producer of tin. Burma is a top producer of rubies. Brunei is one of the world's wealthiest countries as a result of its extensive supplies of oil. Oil exploration has also begun in Vietnam, Cambodia, and the Philippines. Many of the region's natural resources have not yet been fully exploited.

Major industries in the region include the manufacture of computers and electronic components, oil processing, machine and vehicle manufacture, mining, and handicrafts. Southeast Asia is quickly becoming one of the most popular tourist destinations in the world. Tourism has now become a major regional industry, especially in Thailand and Malaysia.

The tiny country of Brunei is an important producer of petroleum and natural gas. The rig shown below is drilling for oil in Brunei's coastal waters.

Energy and power

In those countries with large reserves of oil and natural gas, such as Brunei, Malaysia, Indonesia, and Burma, these resources provide the major sources of power. In Cambodia, timber is still the main energy resource. There are plans to build a thermo-electric plant and to restore a diesel-electric power station in Cambodia. Hydro-electricity is important in the Philippines, Indonesia, Laos, and Burma. There are also plans to construct a nuclear power station in Indonesia. It is due to be completed by the year 2003.

Trade and transportation

The countries of Southeast Asia have traded with the rest of the world for hundreds of years. From the early centuries A.D., merchants from India and Arabia sailed to the region to trade in spices, silks, jewels, and precious metals. They were followed by traders from the colonial powers of Europe. These early traders took advantage of Southeast Asia's natural resources as well as the many sea-trading routes that led to the region.

ASEAN—regional cooperation

The Association of Southeast Asian Nations (ASEAN) was founded in 1967. Its aim is to promote a sense of regional identity and economic cooperation in the area. Brunei, Indonesia, Malaysia, the Philippines, Singapore, and Thailand are all members. In 1991, the ASEAN nations set up the ASEAN Free Trade Area to encourage better trading links between member countries. This organization is expected to become a full common market within fifteen years, and will probably have become a major world-trading partnership by the next century.

The major trading partners of each Southeast Asian country are indicated on the map below.

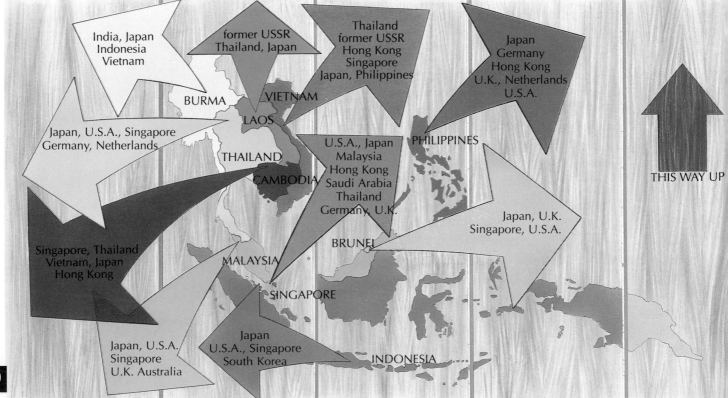

India, Japan Indonesia Vietnam

former USSR Thailand, Japan

Thailand former USSR Hong Kong Singapore Japan, Philippines

Japan Germany Hong Kong U.K., Netherlands U.S.A.

BURMA

VIETNAM

LAOS

Japan, U.S.A., Singapore Germany, Netherlands

THAILAND

PHILIPPINES

U.S.A., Japan Malaysia Hong Kong Saudi Arabia Thailand Germany, U.K.

CAMBODIA

THIS WAY UP

Japan, U.K. Singapore, U.S.A.

Singapore, Thailand Vietnam, Japan Hong Kong

BRUNEI

MALAYSIA

SINGAPORE

Japan, U.S.A. Singapore U.K. Australia

Japan U.S.A., Singapore South Korea

INDONESIA

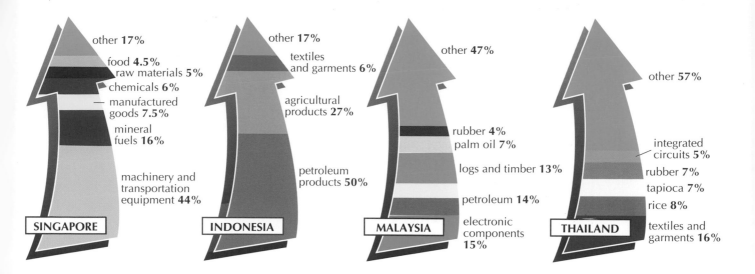

SINGAPORE
other **17%**
food **4.5%**
raw materials **5%**
chemicals **6%**
manufactured goods **7.5%**
mineral fuels **16%**
machinery and transportation equipment **44%**

INDONESIA
other **17%**
textiles and garments **6%**
agricultural products **27%**
petroleum products **50%**

MALAYSIA
other **47%**
rubber **4%**
palm oil **7%**
logs and timber **13%**
petroleum **14%**
electronic components **15%**

THAILAND
other **57%**
integrated circuits **5%**
rubber **7%**
tapioca **7%**
rice **8%**
textiles and garments **16%**

A traditional floating market in northern Thailand. River transportation is a common means of local transportation in the region, particularly in rural areas.

ASEAN also encourages foreign investment in industry. Japan is now the leading trading partner and foreign investor for many Southeast Asian countries, especially Singapore, Indonesia, Malaysia, Thailand, and the Philippines. Many foreign countries, including Japan, have opened factories in Southeast Asia.

Travel and transportation

The transportation network throughout Southeast Asia is closely linked to trade. The great port cities of Singapore, Penang, Rangoon, Jakarta, Saigon (now called Ho Chi Minh City), and Bangkok grew quickly during the colonial era to enable exports to leave the region. Today, Singapore is the world's second largest port, after Rotterdam in the Netherlands.

The road and railway network is spread unevenly across the region, and its quality varies considerably from one area to another. In many countries, roads and railways are restricted to cities and coastal areas. If inland roads exist, they are usually unsurfaced. In both Cambodia and Vietnam, much of the transportation system was destroyed during the recent wars.

Many countries, including Burma, still rely on traditional forms of transportation, such as boats along the rivers. Efforts are now being made to improve the region's transportation network, particularly to reach the more remote areas. Thailand and Singapore already have two of the best international airlines in the world.

A breakdown of the different exports (above) from the region's four main trading nations: Singapore, Indonesia, Malaysia, and Thailand.

Rural changes

Most of the countries in Southeast Asia have economies that are based largely on agriculture. Traditionally, the majority of people have lived in countryside villages and earned their living as farmers and fishermen. This way of life is still predominant throughout much of the region. The exceptions are Singapore and Brunei, where agriculture is less important and more people live in cities than in rural areas.

Tribal culture

Among the hundreds of different ethnic groups who live in Southeast Asia, there are many small tribal groups. These tribal peoples live in remote parts of the countryside, often in forest and mountainous areas. They include the Hmong and Meo of Thailand, the Dayak of Sarawak, and the Karen and Palaung-wa of Burma. Half a million tribal people live in the hills of Thailand alone.

A woman of the Karen tribe. The Karen tribespeople live mostly in the hills that form the border between Burma and Thailand.

Many of these tribes practice a type of farming called slash-and-burn. This means that they clear a plot of land by cutting down and burning the vegetation. They farm the cleared land until all the minerals in the soil are used up. Then they move to another plot of land and clear it in the same way.

Today, the traditional way of life of the tribal peoples is under threat. First, their homes are being destroyed to clear space for settled farms and homes. Second, the countries in which they live are becoming rapidly industrialized.

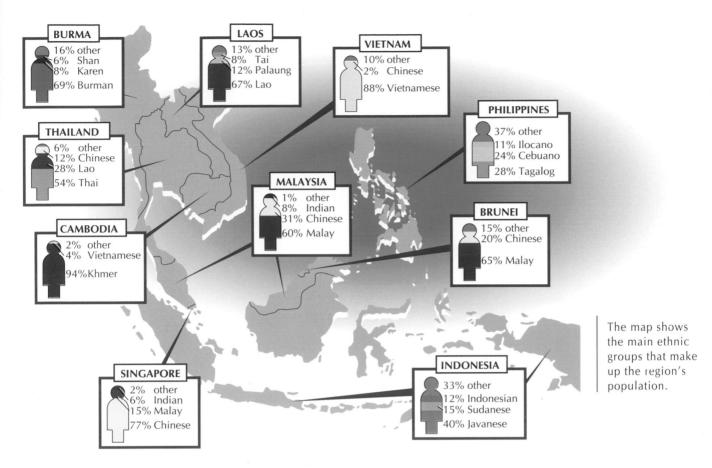

BURMA
16% other
6% Shan
8% Karen
69% Burman

LAOS
13% other
8% Tai
12% Palaung
67% Lao

VIETNAM
10% other
2% Chinese
88% Vietnamese

PHILIPPINES
37% other
11% Ilocano
24% Cebuano
28% Tagalog

THAILAND
6% other
12% Chinese
28% Lao
54% Thai

MALAYSIA
1% other
8% Indian
31% Chinese
60% Malay

BRUNEI
15% other
20% Chinese
65% Malay

CAMBODIA
2% other
4% Vietnamese
94% Khmer

SINGAPORE
2% other
6% Indian
15% Malay
77% Chinese

INDONESIA
33% other
12% Indonesian
15% Sudanese
40% Javanese

The map shows the main ethnic groups that make up the region's population.

A changing countryside

Traditional life elsewhere in the countryside has undergone many changes in recent years. The Communist government in Vietnam forced people off their traditional, family-run farms to work on large, state-owned communes. They were not allowed to own land nor to sell their own crops. The communes were extremely unpopular. Today, people are being allowed to return to their farms.

Changes are taking place across the region in farming technology, too. Although traditional farming methods are still widespread, modern machinery and more productive strains of crops are being introduced. Both help farmers to increase their harvests. Unfortunately, because of the growing population in countries such as Malaysia and Indonesia, more and more land is needed for housing and industry. Traditional farmers are being forced off their own small farms, by groups of wealthy landowners, to work for very low wages on other people's land.

A Dayak longhouse on the island of Borneo. The Dayak people are mainly farmers. Up to 50 families, each with their own room, can live in a single longhouse. The house may be as much as 984 feet (300 m) long.

Urban explosion

Although the majority of people in Southeast Asia still live in the countryside, city populations are growing fast. According to United Nations figures, the urban population in 1950 was 15 percent of the total. By the year 2000, it will have risen to 36 percent. The three largest cities in the region—Bangkok, Manila, and Jakarta—have populations of 5.6 million, 6.7 million, and 7.9 million, respectively. It is estimated that these figures will rise to 11 million, 13 million, and 17 million by the year 2000. These cities will then rank among the world's 30 biggest cities.

The size of the capitals and major cities of Southeast Asia can be seen on the map (below).

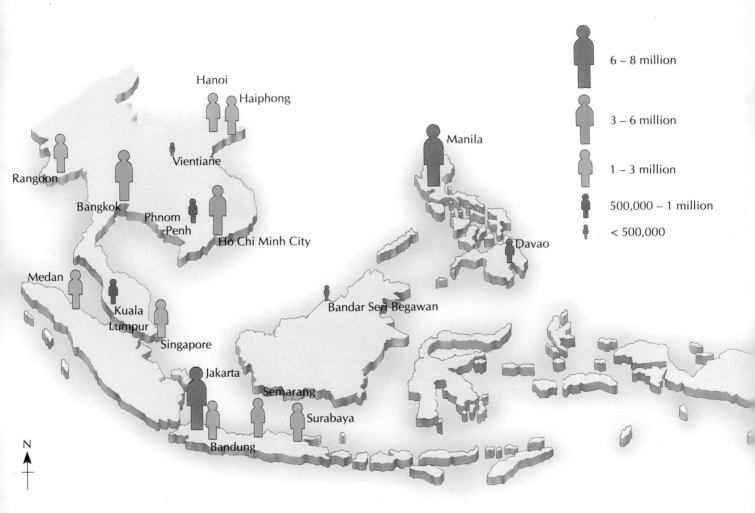

6 – 8 million

3 – 6 million

1 – 3 million

500,000 – 1 million

< 500,000

Hanoi

Haiphong

Vientiane

Manila

Rangoon

Bangkok

Phnom Penh

Ho Chi Minh City

Davao

Medan

Kuala Lumpur

Bandar Seri Begawan

Singapore

Jakarta

Semarang

Surabaya

Bandung

N

The major cities in Southeast Asia are mainly ports and centers of trade that grew in size and importance during colonial times. They are crowded, bustling places with a great mixture of architecture. Building styles range from traditional temples, to colonial buildings, to modern high-rise office and apartment blocks.

Looking for opportunity

The main reason for the rapid growth of Southeast Asia's cities is the large numbers of people arriving from the countryside in search of work. But the cities are unable to cope with this influx of people. Many of the newcomers find themselves without work, or with only occasional, badly paid work. They are forced to live in crowded shanty towns on the edges of the cities. Over one-third of the region's urban population lives in shanty towns and slums.

Transmigration

The Indonesian government has adopted a policy of "transmigration" to deal with the overcrowding of cities such as Jakarta. People are being strongly encouraged to move out of the cities to rural, less-populated areas in, for example, Kalimantan (the Indonesian area of Borneo) and Irian Jaya. It is highly controversial whether this policy is successful.

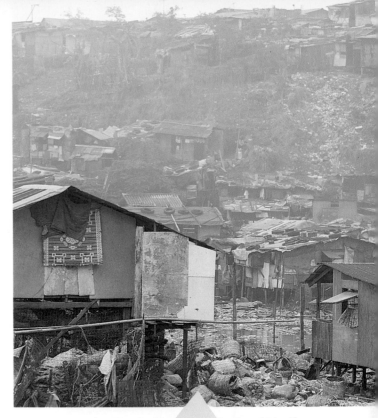

The "Smoky Mountain" district of Manila, capital of the Philippines. Local people live among the rubbish and make a living by sorting it for resale. The piles of burning rubbish surround their homes continuously with smoke, giving this district its name.

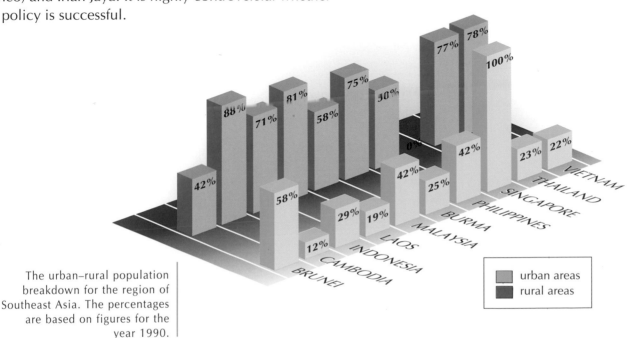

The urban–rural population breakdown for the region of Southeast Asia. The percentages are based on figures for the year 1990.

urban areas
rural areas

BRUNEI 42% / 58%
CAMBODIA 88% / 12%
INDONESIA 71% / 29%
LAOS 81% / 19%
MALAYSIA 58% / 42%
BURMA 75% / 25%
PHILIPPINES 50% / 0%
SINGAPORE 77% / 0%
THAILAND 78% / 23%
VIETNAM 100% / 22%

Landscape under threat

Various environmental problems face the countries of Southeast Asia. The most serious one involves the destruction of the tropical rain forests that used to cover much of the region. The animals and plants of the rain forests are under severe threat. Also, the way of life of the many tribes of people who have lived there for thousands of years is now in danger.

Deforestation danger

Southeast Asia has the third largest area of rain forest in the world, after South America and Africa. It is among the richest natural habitats on earth and is home to thousands of species of plants and animals. Timber products, such as teak, ebony, and other hardwoods, come from the rain forest. They are extremely important earners of foreign revenue for many Southeast Asian countries. But these countries are paying a high price for their foreign earnings.

The tropical rain forest is being destroyed at such an alarming rate that there may be very little left in ten years' time. Many animal species, such as the Bali tiger and Schomburgk's deer, have already become extinct. Many others are in serious danger because of the loss of their habitat. In an effort to save the remaining forests, several countries, including Indonesia, Cambodia, Laos, and Malaysia, have imposed restrictions or even total bans on logging activities and timber exports. Illegal logging still continues, however, despite such bans.

Deforestation has caused widespread damage to the land in the Sarawak and Sabah region of Malaysia (above).

Huge areas of the tropical rain forest that once covered so much of Southeast Asia have now been destroyed (see right). Polluted rivers are another of the region's key environmental problems.

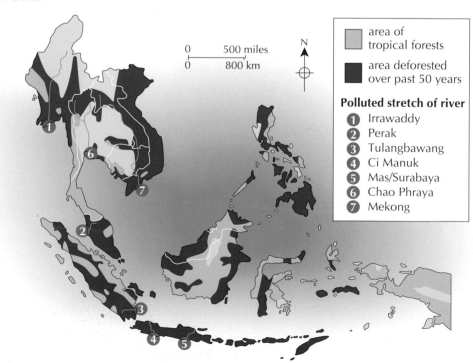

0 ___ 500 miles
0 ___ 800 km

N

■ area of tropical forests

■ area deforested over past 50 years

Polluted stretch of river
1 Irrawaddy
2 Perak
3 Tulangbawang
4 Ci Manuk
5 Mas/Surabaya
6 Chao Phraya
7 Mekong

Conservation efforts

Conservation has become a top priority for the ASEAN nations. They are working together with international environmental groups such as the World Wide Fund for Nature. There have been some important successes. The Vietnamese landscape, for example, was badly damaged during the war. Now it is gradually recovering, and new national parks have been set up. In the early 1990s, two new animal species—a type of ox and a giant muntjac deer—were discovered in Vu Quang Nature Reserve in northern Vietnam.

In Indonesia, over 9 percent of the land is now protected, and 10 percent in Thailand. Several special reserves have been established on Borneo to protect the island's endangered orangutans.

Some examples of rare or endangered wildlife (and their location) in Southeast Asia.

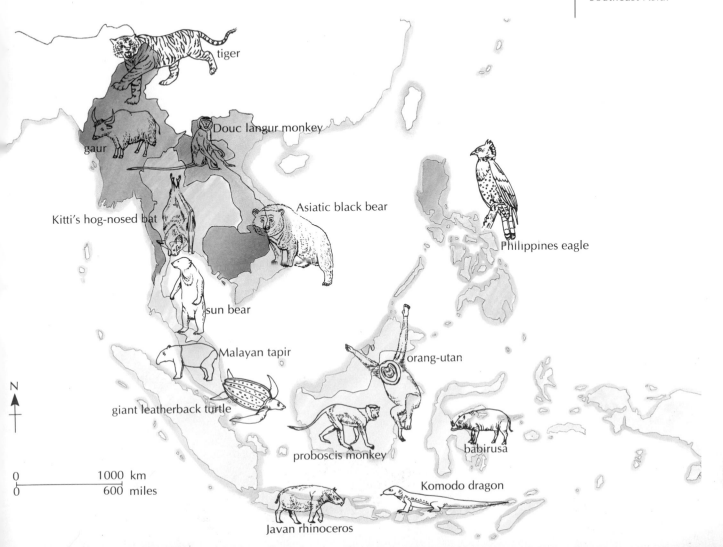

tiger

Douc langur monkey

gaur

Kitti's hog-nosed bat

Asiatic black bear

Philippines eagle

sun bear

Malayan tapir

orang-utan

giant leatherback turtle

proboscis monkey

babirusa

Komodo dragon

Javan rhinoceros

N

0   1000 km
0   600 miles

Facing the future

After centuries of conflict and colonial rule, Southeast Asia is now emerging as one of the fastest growing economies in the world. The ten nations of Southeast Asia have much to look forward to, but there are still problems to be faced. While some people have become rich as a result of trade, the majority of Southeast Asians remain poor.

There is an enormous gulf between the prosperous nations of Singapore, Malaysia, and Brunei and countries such as Laos, Vietnam, Cambodia, and Burma, which are among the poorest in the world. Future economic growth needs to be managed carefully so that more people can benefit from it.

Many refugee camps remain scattered across the region. The people living in these camps are under the care of international organizations such as the Red Cross.

A modern luxury skyscraper hotel towers over the nearby shanty dwelling of a poor family in Jakarta, Indonesia.

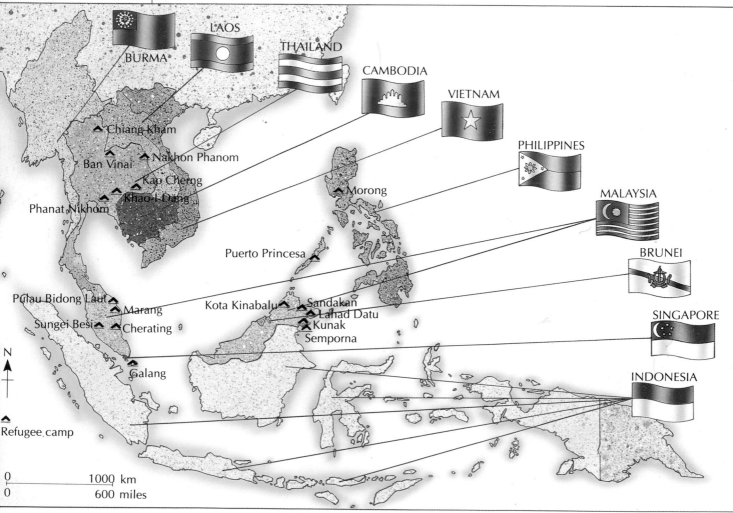

BURMA

LAOS

THAILAND

CAMBODIA

VIETNAM

PHILIPPINES

MALAYSIA

BRUNEI

SINGAPORE

INDONESIA

▲ Chiang Kham

▲ Nakhon Phanom
▲ Ban Vinai

▲ Kap Cheng
▲ Khao-I-Dang
Phanat Nikhom

▲ Morong

Puerto Princesa

Pulau Bidong Laut ▲
▲ Marang
Sungei Besi ▲   ▲ Cherating

Kota Kinabalu ▲   ▲ Sandakan
▲ Lahad Datu
▲ Kunak
Semporna

Galang

N

▲
Refugee camp

0   1000 km
0   600 miles

Refugees and human rights

In the 1960s and 1970s, thousands of people were killed in the wars in Vietnam, Laos, and Cambodia. Thousands more of the inhabitants of these countries became refugees. Some 80,000 Vietnamese and 100,000 Cambodians fled to refugee camps on the border with Thailand.

It is estimated that there are still around 300,000 Vietnamese, Laotians, and Cambodians in refugee camps in Southeast Asia. Their countries remain unstable, and they are too afraid to return to their homes. But the refugees cannot stay in the camps forever. Their governments will have to find ways of tackling the refugee problem.

The governments of several Southeast Asian countries need to resolve other issues involving people's rights. For example, in 1975 the Indonesians invaded the island of East Timor. Tens of thousands of islanders died in the conflict. Since then, the people of East Timor have remained under the harsh rule of the Indonesian government. The United Nations does not recognize Indonesia's takeover of East Timor. But without the involvement of the outside world, the culture and identity of East Timor could be lost.

Many Cambodians have fled from the fighting in their own country to the safety of refugee camps (above) in neighboring Thailand.

Looking forward

Another of Southeast Asia's problems is its rapidly growing population. If this population growth is controlled and the region's other problems are tackled, Southeast Asia faces a bright future. ASEAN has a crucial role to play in this future. It can bring the various countries closer together and encourage them to work toward creating a greater sense of regional identity.

Databank

Physical geography

- The biggest country, by area, in Southeast Asia is Indonesia; Singapore is the smallest.

Brunei	2,225 sq m (5,765 sq km)
Burma	261,322 sq m (677,000 sq km)
Cambodia	69,880 sq m (181,035 sq km)
Indonesia	740,905 sq m (1,919,443 sq km)
Laos	91,405 sq m (236,800 sq km)
Malaysia	127,573 sq m (330,500 sq km)
Philippines	115,800 sq m (300,000 sq km)
Singapore	240 sq m (622 sq km)
Thailand	198,062 sq m (513,115 sq km)
Vietnam	128,036 sq m (331,700 sq km)

- The largest lake in Southeast Asia is Tonle Sap (the Great Lake) in Cambodia. At its fullest, after the monsoon rains, it covers an area of 3,860 square miles (10,000 sq km).
- In 1883, the volcanic island of Krakatoa, situated between Java and Sumatra, erupted with the loudest bang ever heard.
- The outstanding natural beauty of Thailand's countryside has helped to make tourism the country's largest source of foreign earnings.
- Singapore is made up of the densely populated Singapore Island, where most people live, and more than 50 much smaller, neighboring islets.

People

- In 1992, the population and annual growth rate figures for Southeast Asia were:

	population (millions)	growth rate (%)
Brunei	0.27	3.2
Burma	43.7	2.2
Cambodia	9.0	2.7
Indonesia	184.3	1.8
Laos	4.3	2.9
Malaysia	18.6	2.5
Philippines	64.2	2.3
Singapore	2.8	1.8
Thailand	57.9	1.7
Vietnam	69.2	2.3

- Malaysia has one official language: Bahasa Malaysia; Chinese, Tamil, and English are also widely spoken. Indonesia has one official language: Bahasa Indonesia. The Philippines has two official languages, Pilipino and English, and over 70 different dialects.
- The people of Brunei enjoy a high standard of health care. A flying doctor service treats people in isolated locations.
- The population of Southeast Asia is expected to double over the next 35 years. In Thailand and Indonesia, however, strong family planning programs have been set up by the government. These programs have helped to slow the rate of population growth slightly.
- Since 1975, about 800,000 people from Vietnam, Laos, and Cambodia have settled in the U.S., 250,000 in China, and 100,000 each in Canada, France, and Australia.

- In the 1970s, it was estimated that Cambodia's population actually fell from 7 million to 5 million because of the atrocities committed by the Khmer Rouge and because of the mass exodus of refugees.

Currencies

- The currencies of Southeast Asia are:

Brunei	1 dollar = 100 cents
Burma	1 kyat = 100 pyas
Cambodia	1 riel = 100 sen
Indonesia	1 rupiah = 100 sen
Laos	1 kip = 100 at
Malaysia	1 ringgit = 100 sen
Philippines	1 peso = 100 centavos
Singapore	1 dollar = 100 cents
Thailand	1 baht = 100 satang
Vietnam	1 dong = 100 xu

Economy

- The Sultan of Brunei is one of the richest men in the world.
- After years of Communist rule, the governments of Vietnam and Laos are now introducing policies to encourage foreign investment and private businesses. In Vietnam, the policy is called *doi moi*, which means "renovation"; in Laos, it is called *chin thanakan mai*, or "new thinking."
- Agriculture is the principal economic activity in much of Southeast Asia. The proportion of each country's workforce that is employed in agriculture is:

Brunei	4%
Burma	65%
Cambodia	70%
Indonesia	51%
Laos	72%
Malaysia	34%
Philippines	48%
Singapore	1%
Thailand	73%
Vietnam	62%

- As a result of the Vietnam War, Vietnam was littered with abandoned and bombed-out military vehicles and machinery. It is now the world's leading supplier of scrap metal.
- Elephants are such valuable working animals in Southeast Asia that there is even an elephant-training university at Ban Pangha in Thailand. It was set up by the Thailand Forestry Service.

Environment

- The world's largest lizard, the Komodo dragon, lives only on the Indonesian island of Komodo and some smaller neighboring islands. The dragon can grow to be up to 10 feet (3 m) long.
- The Vietnamese landscape, especially in the south, was seriously damaged by chemicals and poisonous gases that were used during the Vietnam War. It is also pitted with thousands of bomb craters.

Glossary

archipelago
A large group of islands, such as those which make up Indonesia.

cash crop
A crop that is grown for sale and for export abroad.

commune
A large state-owned and state-controlled farm established by the Communist government in Vietnam.

delta
An area of low-lying land that forms where a river flows into the sea.

dialect
A variation of a language that is spoken by a few people in a small area.

hydroelectric power
Electricity which is made from the energy produced by fast-flowing water.

irrigation
Taking water from rivers and dams to farmland where it is needed. The water is moved along canals, channels, and pipes.

landlocked
Surrounded by land on all sides.

monsoon
A wind which blows across Asia and changes direction according to the time of year. It can bring heavy rains.

natural resource
Any material which is found naturally in a country, such as tin, oil, timber, etcetera.

paddy field
A field where rice is grown, covered by water at certain times.

palm oil
Oil extracted from the fruit of oil palm trees.

peninsula
A long, thin stretch of land almost surrounded on three sides by sea.

plantation
A large estate on which cash crops, such as rubber, cotton, palm oil, or tobacco are grown.

plate
A section of the outer layers that surround the earth.

refugee
A person who has been forced to flee from his or her own country because of war or for religious or political reasons.

sediment
Fertile mud and soil which are deposited by a river.

source
The place where a river begins, often as a spring high up on a mountainside.

staple food
One of the main types of basic foods eaten by people, such as rice, breads, and potatoes.

trench
A very deep valley in the ocean floor. Trenches are found near the edges of the earth's plates.

typhoon
A violent tropical storm, which brings high winds and heavy rain.

Index